HUGLESS DOUGLAS

David Melling

Z Z Z Z Z Z Z Z Z Z z z z

Hodder Children's Books

One spring morning a big yaaawwwwn came from the back of a deep dark cave.

It was a young brown bear and his name was Douglas.

So he wriggled out
of his pyjamas,

brushed his hair,

put on a scarf
and went to look for one.

'My best hugs are BIG,' thought Douglas so he went up to the biggest thing he could find, wrapped his arms all the way around and gave it a squeeze.

It didn't feel quite right.

'Oooh!' grunted Douglas.
'It's a bit too...

OOF!

...heavy!'

'My best hugs are TALL,' thought Douglas.

So he went up to the tallest thing he could find.

He hugged
the bottom…

he hugged
around the
middle…

and he hugged
as high as he
could reach.

But it was all wrong. And it had splinters.

'My best hugs are comfy,' thought Douglas
and he trotted towards a cosy-looking bush.

He cuddled the bush but something felt very odd.
The leaves *quivered* and *trembled*...

...and ran away!

'GIVE US A HUG!' cried Douglas.

'No!' baa-ed the sheep, 'we're too busy.'

He scooped up armfuls anyway
and tried to cuddle them gently,
but they kicked and squirmed
and didn't like it at all.

Poor
Douglas!

'WHY
CAN'T
I FIND
A
HUG?'
he said.

'If I want a hug,'
said a wise owl,
'I sit in my tree
and –'

'Let me try!' whooped Douglas and he scrambled up next to the owl. But he soon found himself in a clumsy muddle.

'Twooooooooo Twit!' said the owl crossly.

'I only wanted
a hug,' sniffed
Douglas. 'Perhaps
there's one down here?'
He felt something
long-eared and rabbity
and gave it a tug.

Douglas could tell the rabbit didn't want a hug.
He sniffed again and, without thinking, wiped
his nose on the fluffy end.

'Excuuuuse me!' shouted the rabbit. 'Put me down!'

'**BUT I NEED A HUG,**' said Douglas,
'and I can't find one anywhere.'

'Oh, I see,' said the rabbit kindly.
'Come with me.'

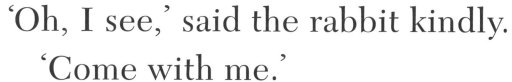

She took Douglas by the paw…

…and led him round and about.

At last they came to a deep dark cave where a sleepy someone was just waking up.

'YAAAWWWWW

Douglas peeped inside. He had the funniest feeling that he knew the someone very well.

'HUG?' asked Douglas,
and ran as fast as
he could towards…

...his MUM!

'Come to think of it, my best hugs are from someone I love,' said Douglas. And he snuggled into the biggest, warmest arms he knew.

Sandwich Hug

Goodnight Hug

Upside-Down Hug

Don't-let-Go Hug

Falling Hug

Shy Hug

Group Hug

Back-to-Front Hug

Solo Hug

Tummy Hug

Daisy-Chain Hug

Big Hug

Come-and-Get-it Hug

Unrequited Hug

Hug Time!
Get Ready To Hug

1. Stretch Out Your Arms **2. Smile** **3. And Squeeze...**

Some of the best hugs are with your family and friends, but you can hug anything really just like Douglas! Who do you like to hug?

Try practising some of the hugs from the hug gallery. Find a friend and try a twisty **Back-To-Front Hug.** Squeeze really tightly for a brilliant **Don't-Let-Go Hug.**

Can you think of your own special hug? Why don't you draw a picture of it and colour it in?

Back-To-Front Hug **Don't-Let-Go Hug**

Remember Hugs Are Very Special To Douglas And To All Of Us!